Riffing Through the Eighties

Short Stories Inspired by the Rock Anthems of the 1980's

Freshwater Horizon Press

Texas

To my wife who takes me back to the 80's every day!

SETLIST:

1. **Knowing It's Right**. Inspired by "Waiting for a Girl Like You" – Foreigner
2. **I'll Be Watching You**. Inspired by "Every Breath You Take" – The Police
3. **Lights**. Inspired by "Don't Stop Believing" - Journey
4. **Last Exit to Memphis**. Inspired by "Here I Go Again" - Whitesnake
5. **A New Verse**. Inspired by "Sweet Child O' Mine" – Guns N' Roses
6. **Halfway There**. Inspired by "Livin' on a Prayer" - Bon Jovi
7. **Silence and Thunder.** Inspired by "In the Air Tonight"– Phil Collins
8. **Between The Lines**. Inspired by "I want to Know What Love Is" - Foreigner
9. **No One Rides for Free.** Inspired by "Wanted Dead or Alive" – Bon Jovi
10. **Last Call**. Inspired by "Have a Drink on Me" – AC/DC

Knowing It's Right

Inspired by "Waiting for a Girl Like You" -
Foreigner

The bell above the door jingled—a soft, metallic chime that cut through the low hum of Miles Davis spinning on the vintage turntable behind the counter.

Jack Hart looked up from his worn stool at the back of "Jack of Hearts Records" blinking behind wire-framed glasses. Outside, rain whispered against the windows, and the October sky had long since dimmed into its gray cloak. The shop was warm with the smell of old cardboard sleeves, pine cleaner, and coffee. Business had been slow for months, not that he minded. He liked the silence. He needed it. This was the life he chose. He was living his dream.

But when the door opened and she walked in, silence took on a different shape.

She wasn't just anyone.

She was Lena.

Twenty years older, yes—but still Lena. Same graceful way of moving. Same chestnut waves framing that sharp, thoughtful face. She paused just inside the door, unsure, dripping rainwater onto the worn welcome mat. Then her eyes met his—and lingered.

Jack's breath caught somewhere behind his ribs.

"Lena?" he asked, as if he might be wrong, as if she might vanish if he sounded too certain.

Her lips parted. "Jack?"

The record skipped slightly. The pre-echo caused by the stylus picking up signals from adjacent grooves... a sound that he loved... yet, at this moment, was the furthest thing from his mind.

Jack stood slowly, steadying himself against the counter. "I... wow. It's been—"

"Years," she finished. "A long time."

She crossed the room, eyes taking in the rows of bins, the posters, the handwritten signs that hadn't changed since the Clinton administration.

"I didn't know you were still here," she said.

"I never left," he said with a wry smile. "And you...?"

"Here for a few days. My aunt passed. I'm helping my cousin clear out her house." She paused. "I thought this place would be gone."

"Nearly was. Twice. But vinyl came back around, like all the best things."

She gave a small smile and nodded toward a display bin. "Still have that copy of I'd Rather Go Blind?"

"Probably three."

They stood in silence for a beat too long.

Lena tucked a strand of hair behind her ear. "Well... I should let you get back to work."

Jack shook his head. "I don't really work. I mostly listen."

She hesitated. "Would it be alright if I browsed a little?"

"Of course."

She drifted through the aisles like a ghost from his past, her fingertips brushing spines of LPs like pages in a diary. Jack tried not to stare. He failed.

The next day, she came back.

It wasn't raining this time, but the sky remained heavy. Lena walked in just as Jack flipped over a sign that read Back in Five Minutes, even though he hadn't left.

"Forget something yesterday?" he asked, casual as he could. He was hoping he would see her again.

She held up a sticky note. "List of albums my cousin wanted. Thought I'd try my luck."

Jack reached under the counter and pulled out two of them before she finished reading the first title aloud.

"Still sharp," she said.

He shrugged. "Still obsessive."

She lingered. Browsed. Talked more than the day before. Laughed once or twice—low, and warm—and Jack felt something in his chest shift. He almost had to hold his chest but didn't. She told him about her daughter, just started college. About the divorce, two years old but still leaving bruises.

He didn't mention the years he spent alone, or the handful of short-lived relationships that never touched the part of him still haunted by her. Instead, he brewed them both some coffee in the backroom and returned with two mismatched mugs.

"Do you remember," Lena said as she sipped, "when we used to dance in your dorm room? That tiny little record player you had?"

He chuckled. "It barely played. Sounded like someone whispering through soup."

"I didn't care. I just liked that you always knew what song to put on."

She looked up.

"I waited for you, you know. After graduation."

Jack stared down into his cup. "I know."

"You said you'd come to Denver."

"I know."

Her eyes were kind, not angry. "Why didn't you?"

He let out a breath. "I was scared. Scared I'd hold you back. You had dreams, Lena. Big ones. I just had records."

"That was enough for me," she said, softly.

It was a nice thing to say, but it was also haunting and cold. That night, Jack couldn't sleep. He shuffled through a crate in the store's backroom marked "Personal" until he found it: the faded Foreigner album she'd once called cheesy in the best way. He brushed off the dust, set it on the turntable, and dropped the needle.

As Waiting for a Girl Like You filled the store, he turned the volume up—not too loud, just enough. He must have heard the song a thousand times because the morning light was starting to make an appearance as it peered through the store windows. Letting the song play on, he cleaned himself up, changed and opened for business. He loved that his place was above his shop.

In what seemed like a few seconds later, the bell jingled over the music. Lena stepped inside and smiled like she already knew.

"I'm leaving tomorrow," she said, "but I'd love to see you one last time. Maybe dinner?"

Jack hesitated. He hadn't had dinner with anyone since his mother's funeral. His instinct was to retreat. But instead, he nodded.

"Yes. I'd like that."

They met at a small Italian place just off Main Street. She wore a dark green scarf and the same scent he remembered from college—something floral, like lavender and nostalgia.

They talked for hours. About her life. About his. About regrets and roads not taken.

At one point, she reached across the table and touched his hand.

"I always thought you were the love of my life," she said.

Jack didn't flinch. "I thought I was just the first chapter."

"You were more than that," she whispered. "You still are."

He walked her to her rental car. The rain had returned, light but steady.

"You know," she said, "I've been thinking about staying. Not forever. But maybe for a while."

Jack's heart beat faster than it had in years.

"Why?" he said, trying to be cool, calm... maybe even smooth.

She smiled. "Because for the first time in a long time, I feel like I'm where I'm supposed to be."

He nodded. "I'd like that."

She leaned in and kissed him on the cheek. "Goodnight, Jack."

"Goodnight, Lena."

The next day, Jack opened the shop late.

He flipped the "Closed" sign around and turned on the lights. The store smelled like rain and hope.

He pulled out the Foreigner record again and let it play.

As the first notes filled the room, he moved between the aisles, adjusting sleeves, humming softly.

Then the door opened.

And Lena stepped in, holding two cups of coffee and a shy smile.

"I figured you might not have made any yet," she said.

Jack took a cup, their fingers brushing.

"No," he said. "But I was waiting... hoping even."

"The wait is over Jack," she said as she smiled, set her cup down, and motioned him to dance with her.

THE END

I'll Be Watching You

Inspired by "Every Breath You Take" -The Police

The camera lens barely moved.

Just a slight tilt, a gentle zoom, and the image became clear: a man on a balcony, glass of wine in hand, laughing with someone out of frame. He ran his fingers through his own hair, pushing it back from his forehead. His beaming smile placed perfectly on his face. His eyes, playful, as if he wasn't being watched. Like the world wasn't recording.

But it was. She was.

Ten Luna adjusted the focus. Ten was short for Hortencia... a name she dropped when opening her PI firm almost a decade ago. She'd been sitting in her black sedan for three hours, parked under a dying streetlamp. It was the kind of job she could do in her sleep by now—divorce cases, cheating wives, secret girlfriends. Always the same.

But this one was different.

This one was him.

His name was Jess Lucian. Thirty-two. Music teacher. Married to a wealthy finance exec who believed he was having an affair. He was, according to the client's suspicions, "sneaky, flirtatious, and a complete player."

Ten had taken the job without hesitation.

Then she'd seen him.

And the job changed.

The first night, she followed him from a cigar shop to a bookstore. He sat by the window, drank coffee and read. His fingers wrapped around his ceramic mug like it held memories. The streetlight caught his face just enough to show the faint scar near his eyebrow. She found herself wondering how he got it.

The second night, he walked his dog—an old goldendoodle named Sadie. He stopped to help a kid fix his bike chain. The kid was thankful and gave Jess a huge high-five before he left. Ten watched from across the street, invisible.

The third night, he sang. The sound traveled through an open window. She couldn't make out the tune, but his voice was strong and haunted, like someone remembering a love that never came back.

She recorded every movement. Every step. Every breath.

But the tapes weren't for the client anymore.

They were for her.

Ten told herself it was professional. She logged his locations, tagged timestamps, and wrote summaries like she always did. But her reports were vague. Incomplete. She never mentioned the way he laughed when he was alone. Or how he looked vulnerable when watching old black-and-white movies. She never mentioned the woman in the balcony chair.

Because there was no woman.

Jess was alone.

It had been seventeen nights when Ten crossed the line.

He left his apartment late—around 11:45 PM—and walked toward the corner liquor store. He wore sweats and a t-shirt that complemented his muscular physique. Hoodie over his head. Prepared for the rain just starting to fall, he opened his umbrella.

Ten followed on foot this time.

She stayed in the shadows, her camera bag slung over her shoulder. He walked with his head down, music in his ears. He passed a woman sitting on the curb, gave her his umbrella, and kept walking through the rain like he didn't notice.

He went inside the store. Ten waited.

When he came out, he paused.

Then turned.

Looked directly at her.

"I saw you," he said.

Ten froze.

His voice wasn't angry. Just... steady.

"I've seen you. The car. The alley. The cigar shop. For two weeks now."

She swallowed. "I—"

He held up a hand. "Let me guess. My wife?"

"...Yes."

Jess sighed, licked his lips, not because they were dry, but out of habit, and stared at her.

"What did she tell you I was doing?"

Ten hesitated. "Cheating."

He scoffed. "Of course."

"Are you?"

He stepped closer. "Why? Would that make this easier for you to justify?"

The rain pelted around them, the neon sign from the liquor store blinking red across his face.

"Do you enjoy watching people?" he asked. "Knowing things they don't know you know?"

Ten wanted to say no. But the lie wouldn't come.

"I used to," she said nervously.

He looked at her for a long time.

"You look sad," he finally said, slightly touching her shoulder.

That surprised her more than anything.

He walked away.

And Ten didn't follow.

She returned home that night and watched the tapes. Every frame. Every pause. She studied his face like it held a secret only she could learn if she just stared long enough. But it wasn't love. It wasn't admiration.

It was loneliness.

His. Hers. Twisting together.

The next morning, she called the client.

"He's not cheating," Ten said.

There was a long pause.

"You're sure?"

"Yes. He's... isolated. Sad. But he's not seeing anyone."

The wife grunted. "Then he's just wasting my time."

Ten hung up, tired of the toxic tone coming from the phone.

She deleted the files. Burned the notes.

But she couldn't erase the memory of his voice in the rain.

A week passed.

Then another.

Ten didn't return to his street. She didn't answer calls from clients. She sat in her apartment and thought about the people she had followed over the years. Husbands, wives, lovers, liars.

They blurred together.

Except him.

On the fiftieth night since they talked in the rain, she found herself outside his apartment again.

The lights were off. Curtains drawn.

But she could see his silhouette—alone at the window. Staring out.

He didn't look at her.

Didn't move.

He just stood there.

Like he knew she was watching.

The End

Lights

Inspired by "Don't Stop Believing"
-Journey

The Greyhound pulled out of Fresno just past 10:00 p.m.

The fluorescent lights flickered once overhead before settling into a low hum. Most of the passengers leaned against windows, earphones in, hoodies up. The bus smelled faintly of diesel, cinnamon gum, and unspoken stories.

Monica slouched into seat 17A, duffel bag tucked beneath her feet, guitar case hugged against her chest like armor. She hadn't eaten. Her hands were shaking. But she was finally moving—on the road to Los Angeles.

She didn't believe in signs, but when the bus driver flipped on the intercom and the radio came through for a moment—"Don't stop believin', hold on to that feelin'..."—she had to smile.

"Nice song," came a voice beside her.

She looked up.

A guy, probably her age, maybe a little older—clean hoodie, beat-up sneakers, shaggy hair and green eyes like a faded highway sign. He dropped into 17B and stuck out a hand.

"Name's Celso."

Monica hesitated, then shook it.

"Monica."

They rode in silence for a few miles. Then he asked, "LA or bust?"

"LA," she said. "Maybe bust."

He chuckled. "Same."

She glanced at him. "What are you running from?"

He smirked. "Who said I'm running?"

"You have that 'I left a mess behind' face."

He looked impressed. "You psychic?"

"No. I'm from a town so small, you can hear hearts breaking two blocks away."

They both laughed, and something in Monica's chest unknotted a little.

They talked through Bakersfield.

Celso had been a barback at a club in Reno. Dated the owner's daughter. That didn't end well. Monica had played acoustic sets in coffee shops back in Modesto. She had talent but no connections—and her stepdad had recently told her that music was "a hobby for dreamers, not survivors."

"You disagree?" Celso asked.

"I think people who stop dreaming just start dying slower."

He nodded. "Fair."

By midnight, the bus was quiet. The driver dimmed the lights.

Monica shifted, her head lightly bumping against the window.

Then Celso said, softly, "What's your big dream?"

She was quiet a moment.

"To play one song... just one... in front of a crowd that sings it back to me."

"Damn," he whispered. "That's good."

She looked at him. "You?"

He smiled faintly. "To stop looking over my shoulder."

They pulled into a rest stop around 2:00 a.m.

Monica got out, stretched, bought a Coke and a stale muffin. When she got back on the bus, Celso wasn't in his seat.

She scanned the rows.

Not there.

She waited. Ten minutes passed. Then fifteen.

The driver came back on board.

"We good?"

Monica hesitated, looked toward the restroom area, then nodded.

The bus pulled away.

It wasn't until they were halfway down the interstate that she noticed something in her guitar case's outer pouch.

A folded napkin.

Scrawled in black pen:

"Find what you're chasing. Even if it scares you. – C. G.

P.S. Keep playing. Even when no one's listening. Especially then."

She smiled.

Just a little.

The city lights of Los Angeles were still a couple of hours away, but for the first time in a long time... Monica believed she'd get there.

The End

Last Exit to Memphis

Inspired by "Here I Go Again"
- Whitesnake

They say you can't go home again.

But George Steel didn't have a home anymore—not really. Just a half-dead van, a rusted Les Paul, and a glove compartment full of regrets.

He lit a cigarette with fingers still calloused from chords he hadn't played in months. The wind whipped through the cracked window as he drove south on Highway 55, past fields that used to mean something and signs that pointed everywhere but back.

"Here I go again on my own..." he sang softly, the old Whitesnake lyric floating into the dark. "Goin' down the only road I've ever known."

George used to be somebody.

Lead singer and guitarist for *Martellus*—a bar band that almost broke big. They opened for Ratt once. Had a college radio hit called "Down by the Levi." There were shows, women, long nights and longer dreams.

But the years passed. Labels ghosted them. The bassist, Buddy Pools, found God. The drummer, JT, found rehab. George found the bottom of a bottle.

Now, at 54, all he had was the van, the guitar, and enough gas money to get him as far as Memphis.

He didn't know why he was going there.

Maybe to remember.

Maybe to forget.

It was a dusty little diner in Arkansas that changed everything.

George stopped for coffee and eggs and sat in a booth near the window. He looked like hell—old jeans, leather jacket, ponytail gone mostly gray.

Then he heard her.

A girl at the front counter, humming while waiting on her food. Voice low, rich, gritty—like whiskey through velvet. He was briefly reminded of his younger sister, Yvette, but the girl looked nothing like her.

He perked up.

"You sing?" he asked.

She blinked. "Sometimes."

"What was that you were humming?"

She hesitated, then said, "Fleetwood Mac. Dreams."

George nodded. "Good choice."

32

She looked him over. "You a musician or just another creep who hangs out in diners?"

He smirked. "Little of both."

She laughed.

Her name was Rocio. Twenty-three. Worked nights at the diner. Played open mics when she could. Wanted to move to Nashville but didn't have the nerve—or the cash.

George showed her his guitar. She asked him to play.

He did.

A soft blues riff. Nothing flashy. Just feeling.

When he finished, she stared.

"You used to be big, didn't you?"

George shrugged. "Almost."

They talked for hours. Music. Life. Regrets.

Rocio confessed she was scared. Afraid of failing. Afraid of leaving her mom behind. Afraid of being another voice lost in a crowd.

George understood. Too well.

Then she said, "You ever think about trying again?"

George looked out the window.

"Every damn day."

They left together at dawn.

George didn't know what he was doing. He just knew he wasn't done yet.

They played dive bars down through Mississippi. Her voice, his guitar. The kid at the soundboard in Biloxi said they sounded like "Janis and Clapton's secret lovechild."

They laughed. Cried once. Slept in the van. Ate gas station sandwiches. Lived like they meant it.

And one night in Memphis, they landed a spot at The Last Exit—a legendary hole-in-the-wall where legends were born.

Rocio was nervous.

George looked at her backstage and said, "Don't wait thirty years to figure out you're good enough. Go show them now."

She did.

She killed it.

After the show, Andy Youngman, a well-known producer in Memphis, handed her a card. They talked. Andy learned that she was living in her friend's van. With a quick phone call, he made arrangements and had an assistant book a fancy hotel.

"Call me in the morning," Andy said as he pointed at the card in her hand.

She stared at it for a long time.

Then she looked at George.

"What about you?"

He smiled. "My road's different."

"You sure?"

He looked at the crowd, the lights, the haze of smoke and applause.

Then back at her.

"I've already made it. Watching you shine? That's the encore I never got."

George left town the next morning before she woke up.

No note.

Just his old Les Paul, resting in the back of the van as he drove away.

"Here I go again on my own..."

George sang, driving into the sunrise.

Still moving.

Still dreaming.

Alone, yet with a glimmer of hope.

The End

A New Verse

Inspired by "Sweet Child O' Mine" – Guns N' Roses

The rumble of the Harley echoed through the quiet streets of Clint, Texas like thunder through a church.

Will Powers hadn't been back in over twenty years. Not since the night he left under the glow of red taillights and regret. He told himself back then that he was doing her a favor—that his daughter didn't need a man like him around.

But now she was getting married.

And she'd asked for him.

The town hadn't changed much. Same diners. Same cracked sidewalks. Same tree by the

38

river where he used to carve promises he never kept.

He parked outside the little chapel on Center Street. His leathers creaked as he stepped off the bike. Tattoos snaked up his arms, faded and inked over—like scars with color.

He didn't belong here.

Not anymore.

Inside, people buzzed with last-minute decorations and rehearsal chaos. Then he saw her.

Lily.

She was standing near the altar, clipboard in hand, hair pinned up like she always used to for church. She turned—and froze.

"Will."

"Hey, Lily."

He expected her to slap him. Or cry. Or both.

Instead, she nodded. "She's in the back. Waiting."

"She nervous?"

"She's excited." Lily hesitated. "She wants to sing with you. You still play?"

Will patted the case slung over his back. "Always."

Backstage, his daughter sat cross-legged on a bench in a white rehearsal dress. She looked up, eyes wide, and smiled.

She was the spitting image of Lily. But with his soft eyes.

"You came," she whispered.

Will swallowed. "Course I did, sweetheart."

She stood and hugged him tight. It hit him like a freight train. The years. The silence. The weight of being a ghost in your own bloodline.

"I picked the song," she said, pulling back. "You used to sing it to me when I was little. Mom said you used to hum it before you left."

Will smiled softly. "Sweet Child O' Mine."

At the rehearsal dinner, Will played while his daughter sang. Her voice was shaky but pure. He strummed gently, just enough to guide her through the chorus. The room was quiet.

Even Lily watched with a softness in her stare that cracked something in him.

Later that night, Lily sat with him on the church steps.

"Why did you come back?" she asked.

Will exhaled smoke from a cigarette he never lit.

"She asked."

"She always asked. Every birthday. Every Christmas. Every time she sang that damn song."

Will stared at the moon not able to conceal the years of regret and pain on his face.

"I was afraid. That I'd ruin her."

Lily's voice was sharp now. "You almost ruined her by not being there."

He nodded. "I know," he said with a ton of regret weighing down on him.

Silence.

Then she said, "She forgives you, you know."

Will looked down.

"Do you?"

Lily didn't answer. Not right away.

But she leaned her head gently against his shoulder.

And that was enough.

The next day, Will walked his daughter down the aisle.

His boots thudded against the hardwood. His eyes burned with a thousand things unsaid.

But when he handed her off, she squeezed his hand and whispered:

"Thank you for showing up."

He sat beside Lily during the ceremony.

And when the DJ played Sweet Child O' Mine for the father-daughter dance, Will stepped out onto the floor.

As the dam of tears finally broke from his eyes, he placed one hand in hers... the other finally letting go of the past.

The End

Halfway There

Inspired by "Livin' on a Prayer"   - Bon
                                        Jovi

The rent was due on Friday.

By Thursday night, Tomás had twenty-two bucks in his wallet, a cracked phone with a broken charger, and a half-full tank of gas in the car he barely owned.

Georgina was on the couch, fast asleep, her apron still on, takeout box in her lap. She'd worked two doubles this week at Rosa's Cantina. Last night she slipped on a wet tile and twisted her ankle. Still, she showed up for the breakfast shift.

They hadn't told their parents. Or their friends. Or each other—just how scared they really were.

Tomás stood at the window of their one-room apartment in San Jose, staring out at the city lights beyond the crumbling fire escape. He rubbed his hands together, trying to feel warm even though the heat had been off for two weeks.

They were behind on rent. Again.

Their landlord, Mr. Lazos, had been "nice" the first few times—meaning he didn't change the locks. But this time he taped a red notice to the door with bold black words: FINAL WARNING.

"You okay?"

Geogina's voice, sleepy and soft, from the couch.

Tomás turned. "Yeah."

"Don't lie."

He walked over and kissed her forehead. "I got a plan."

She looked up at him, eyes wide and tired. "Another one?"

"This one's real."

She raised an eyebrow. "Tomás…"

"Trust me."

She gave a faint smile. "Always."

Tomás' plan was simple. And stupid.

Fight night at Los Chicos. Underground. Cash only. Winner takes all.

$5,000.

Enough to pay rent and keep the lights on.

He hadn't fought in two years. Not since he broke his hand and promised Georgina he was done. But promises don't keep the heat on, and it can get cold in San Jose in the middle of December.

The next night, Georgina wrapped his hands in cloth, just like she used to.

"You don't have to do this," she whispered, halfway knowing they truly needed this to work.

"I do," he said.

She looked at him, eyes shimmering. "Just come back to me."

He kissed her once, and left without another word.

The fight was in the back room of a bar that smelled like sweat and old beer. Men shouted. Money changed hands. A ring of men surrounded a cracked cement floor. No ropes. No ref.

Tomás took off his jacket, revealing bruised knuckles and a faded tattoo of Georgina's name near his shoulder.

The guy across from him looked like he chewed bricks for breakfast.

Tomás nodded.

The makeshift bell rang.

It was three rounds of blood, instinct, and memory.

Every time he stumbled, he heard Georgina's voice.

Every time he saw stars, he thought of their apartment. The bills on the table. The broken faucet. The dream.

The life they were building—imperfect, messy, real.

He hit the floor once. Got up before the count of two.

And in the final round, with one lucky hook that came from the strength of his ancestors, he dropped the brick-chewer like a sack of cement.

The room roared, "*Estodo CABRON!*"

But Tomás only heard Georgina's voice.

He walked home, busted lip, black eye, and five thousand dollars in his pocket.

Georgina was sitting on the steps outside, her foot wrapped, a blanket around her shoulders.

He showed her the money.

She stood—painfully—and hobbled into his arms.

"You did it," she whispered.

He held her tight
. "No, we did it."

She laughed through tears. "Still broke. Still behind."

"But we're halfway there," he said, kissing her.

"Livin' on a prayer?"

"Exactly."

That night, they fell asleep on the couch, wrapped in each other, dreaming of something bigger.

Not riches. Not miracles.

Just one more day.

Together.

The End

Silence and Thunder

Inspired by "In the Air Tonight"– Phil Collins

The man at the bar looked like a ghost wrapped in leather.

He sat alone, nursing a scotch that hadn't moved in ten minutes. The jukebox buzzed softly in the background. The same Phil Collins song looping faintly but not from the jukebox... it was coming from a Bluetooth speaker someone forgot to disconnect.

"I can feel it coming in the air tonight, oh Lord..."

He closed his eyes.

He had felt it coming for years.

His name was Robert Carr. Once a cop. Now just a retired nobody living in a lakeside cabin outside of Dallas. No wife. No kids. Just guilt, regret, and the thick silence of memory.

Every year on this day—July 17th—he came to this bar. Sat at the same stool. Ordered the same drink. And waited for the weight of it all to settle again.

Twenty-five years ago, he watched a man drown.

Didn't jump in. Didn't call for help.

Because the man who drowned deserved it.

Or so he told himself.

Tonight, something felt different.

The bar was quieter than usual. Too quiet. A storm was brewing outside, thunder grumbling like distant warning shots. The bartender was new—young, clean-cut, and silent.

Robert studied him. There was something familiar about the kid's eyes.

"You ever lose someone?" Robert asked, voice raspy.

The bartender looked up slowly. "Yeah."

"Someone close?"

"Too close."

Robert took a long drink. "Sorry to hear that."

The bartender wiped a glass that didn't need wiping.

"My dad," he said. "Drowned. When I was a kid."

Robert froze.

The room seemed to darken. The music slowed

in his ears.

"Sorry," Robert muttered again, heart thudding.

"Thing is," the kid continued, "he didn't know how to swim. So, it didn't make sense when they said he decided to take a late-night dip."

Robert stared at him.

"I was there," the kid said. "I saw someone on the dock that night."

Robert's mouth went dry.

"I was only nine, but I remember the shape of his face. The way he stood. Just watched. Then walked away."

Lightning lit up the bar in a violent flash.

"You think he meant to let him die?" Robert asked, trying to stay calm.

The kid's eyes didn't waver. "I don't think. I know."

A long pause.

"Why tell me?" Robert asked.

"Because it's time."

The kid pulled something from his pocket—a small cassette recorder.

"I want to hear you say it."

Robert stared at it.

Everything in him screamed to lie. To run. To disappear into the storm.

But then the song played again. Louder this time.

"Well, if you told me you were drowning, I would not lend a hand..."

He took a breath.

And began to speak.

Robert told the whole story. Sweating. Shaking inside.

How the victim—Richard Colmenero—was a dirty cop who framed people, beat suspects, and got off on power. How he threatened Robert's sister. How Robert warned him. How the lake became a choice.

"I told myself it was justice," Robert said. "But it was vengeance."

When he finished, the kid—Richard's son—just sat there.

Tears welled in his eyes.

He hit STOP on the recorder.

Then slid it into his pocket.

"I've been carrying this weight for twenty-five years," Robert said, voice cracking.

"I know," the kid replied. "Now it's mine."

Outside, the storm broke.

Inside, an even bigger storm of emotions.

Rain poured like judgment. Thunder boomed, mirroring an explosive drum fill.

The kid stood.

"You're not the only ghost in this story," he said.

Then he left.

Robert sat alone in the flickering light. The

thunder was pounding. In between booms... deathly silence. He was not scared. He was relieved almost. But empty. Very empty... as empty as the bar.... just him and the song that never seemed to end.

"I've been waiting for this moment, for all my life..."

The End

Between The Lines

Inspired by "I want to Know What Love Is" - Foreigner

Greg Means had seen love at its worst.

In 27 years as a divorce attorney, he'd heard every lie, betrayal, and petty cruelty imaginable. People fighting over coffee makers and custody weekends. Broken dreams and promises that turned to greed and anger. Empty stares across cherrywood conference tables.

He used to believe in love.

Then he built a career watching it rot.

He was pouring bourbon into his coffee one late November evening when his doctor called.

"Your scan lit up," the voice said.

Lit up. Like fireworks in the dark. Like a fuse with a short burn.

Stage two.

Not terminal—but not nothing either.

Greg sat in the stillness of his high-rise office. Outside, snow threatened to fall. Inside, he stared at a framed photo of a woman he hadn't spoken to in eight years.

His ex-wife.

She'd once said, "I hope someday you figure out what love really is. Not what you fight against in court."

Now, he wondered if she had been right.

Two days later, a new client walked in.

Nataly Reyes. Late 30s. Soft-spoken, with fire tucked behind her eyes.

"I want a clean break," she said, sliding a folder across the table. "No games. No revenge. Just peace."

Greg raised an eyebrow. "That's rare."

"I'm tired," she said. "And I don't want my daughter growing up thinking love has to hurt."

He stared at her for a moment. "You ever think of going back... trying to fix the relationship?"

She shook her head. "You ever think of trying again?" guessing that he was divorced too.

Greg smiled bitterly. "No. Not in years."

Days passed. Something about Nataly lingered.

She wasn't jaded. She wasn't angry.

She was... hopeful. Even through grief. He wondered how she could be that way and almost wished he could do the same.

They met again for follow-up paperwork. Then again to discuss mediation. Then again over coffee at the café below his office.

She laughed easily. She asked him real questions.

And she listened.

One evening, after a long session, she touched his arm and said, "You don't smile much, but when you do—it's honest."

Greg didn't know what to say.

That night, he didn't pour bourbon in his coffee.

The case finalized three weeks later. She came to pick up the paperwork. He handed her the envelope, and she hesitated before leaving.

"You okay?" she asked.

"I've been better," he admitted.

Then he told her—about the scan, the prognosis, the feeling of everything catching up to him at once.

She didn't say, "I'm sorry."

She said, "You've still got time."

The next day, Greg canceled a dozen client calls and drove three hours to see his ex-wife.

They talked. Laughed. Apologized.

He didn't ask for anything back.

He just said, "Thank you. For loving me when I didn't know how to return it."

Weeks later, as the snow finally came down in thick sheets, Greg stood at Nataly's door with two coffees and a small, shaking hope.

She opened it, surprised.

"You said you wanted peace," he said. "I'd like to learn how."

She stepped aside to let him in.

In time, he would.

The End

No One Rides for Free

Inspired by "Wanted Dead or Alive" – Bon Jovi

The sky over El Paso, Texas stretched like an open wound—burning orange on the edges, dark and endless at the center.

Mark Montana rode through it like a ghost on two wheels.

His old Harley coughed with each mile, saddlebag flapping in the wind. The bounty papers were stuffed inside, already wrinkled from sweat and hesitation.

Target: Joey Franco

Charges: Armed robbery, two counts of assault, one dead guard

Bounty: $35,000

Status: Armed. Dangerous. Fleeing.

What the sheet didn't say?

They grew up in the same deprived neighborhood in South-Central El Paso. Pera Avenue. Three short blocks from the border.

Joey had been Mark's best friend once. Practically a brother.

They learned to steal hubcaps and throw knives together. Took beatings side by side. Saved each other's lives more than once—Joey most recently, back in the Marines. A desert ambush. One grenade. One split-second shove.

Joey didn't hesitate.

Now he was on the run, and Mark was being paid to find him.

Mark reached the last known location: a shuttered truck stop in the desert. Blood on the dirt lot. Tire marks. Drag trail.

Mark followed them through mesquite and sand until he spotted a lone shed near the edge of a dried-out arroyo. The door was barely shut.

He dismounted, hand on his sidearm.

Inside, Joey was on the floor, half-conscious, gut wound soaking through a stolen shirt.

He looked up with one bloodshot eye and smiled weakly. "Didn't think you'd come."

Mark holstered his weapon.

"You always did have a habit of showing up late," Joey muttered.

Mark knelt beside him.

"You going to arrest me?"

"Wasn't sure."

"You still sure about anything?"

"No."

Joey coughed, blood flecking his lips.

"I didn't shoot that guard. He surprised us. One of the kids panicked. I ran because no one listens when you've got my record."

Mark stared. "You think I came to judge you?"

Joey squinted. "Then why?"

"I thought maybe if I brought you in... it'd balance something. What you did for me back in Fallujah."

Joey smiled faintly. "No such thing as balance, brother. Just debts and sand."

Outside, the sky darkened. Coyotes called in the

distance.

Mark lit a cigarette, standing in the doorway.

Joey's voice drifted through the silence. "How's your daughter?"

Mark's jaw tightened.

"She's eleven," he said. "Lives in Albuquerque. I send cards."

"She ever write back?"

"No."

A long pause.

"You ever visit?"

"No."

Joey coughed again, sharp and wet.

"You know, Mark... you live like no one owes you. But you owe yourself more than this."

Inside, Joey's eyes fluttered. "You gonna call it in?"

Mark looked at him.

Then at the bounty papers in his hand.

Then at his reflection in the shattered window— an aging outlaw, beard graying, gun heavy, heart heavier. Wasting away.

He thought about all the men he'd dragged in. The ones who fought. The ones who cried. The ones who just looked tired.

He remembered Joey at thirteen, covering for him when Mark stole Valium and Xanax from his mom.

He remembered Joey at twenty-nine, hauling his

body out of fire.

He remembered Joey now—dying, maybe innocent, definitely broken.

Mark dropped the cuffs onto the dirt.

"I'm not calling anyone."

Joey opened one eye. "Then what?"

"I'll wrap your side, patch you up best I can. Head to Juarez. I'll leave a key to the bike on the saddle."

It wouldn't be the first time either one of them hid out across the border. Juarez, Mexico was their backyard when they were kids.

Joey stared. "You know I might not make it."

"You might."

"And you'll lose the money."

Mark's voice was low. "Money's not the only thing you can lose."

By morning, Joey was gone.

So was the bike.

Mark left the bounty envelope burning in a rusted barrel out back... watched it curl and smoke.

He hitched a ride with a rancher heading west. A gang of tumbleweeds were headed east at the same time.

No badge. No bounty. No destination.

Just a small photo of a girl in his wallet.

The End

Last Call

Inspired by "Have a Drink on Me" -
AC/DC

There was only one bar in Tornillo, Texas—and it
wouldn't close until the roosters crowed.

Locals called it *La Rodilla del Diablo* (The
Devil's Knee) because it bent every man who walked
through the door.

By the time Clyde B. Arker staggered in at 11:42
PM, the jukebox was already screaming AC/DC, and
the bartender had one eye on the bottle and the other
on the shift clock.

Clyde looked like a ghost with a hangover—boots
worn thin, leather jacket sweat-stained, and a duffel
bag full of nothing but regrets.

He slid onto a cracked stool and muttered,
"Whiskey. Cheap. Dirty."

The bartender—tall, silver-bearded, and unfazed—poured without a word.

The first shot lit Clyde's throat on fire.

The second numbed the edges of whatever was left of his soul.

He didn't bother with a chaser. Or conversation.

"Rough day?" asked a woman two stools down.

She wore a denim jacket with rhinestones and a knowing smirk. Her name, he'd later learn, was Monica.

"You don't know the half of it," Clyde grunted.

"I can guess. Man walks in alone, carrying a bag he doesn't plan to carry out. That's usually the type."

Clyde glanced at her. "You a fortune teller?"

"No," she said, raising her glass. "Just familiar with the script."

The bar filled with laughter and rowdy music, but Clyde sat still—like a statue on the verge of collapse.

He'd spent the last year losing everything that ever mattered: job, house, wife, driver's license. The last straw was the call from his brother: "Don't come to the funeral. You'd just ruin it."

So he'd driven through the desert with a half-plan: drink until he vanished... get blinded out of his mind.

Monica leaned in. "You look like a man who came to Tornillo to disappear."

Clyde nodded slowly.

"Well, bad news," she said, sipping whiskey, ice, and water. "Nobody disappears here. They just dry up."

He laughed. First time in weeks. "You live here?"

"Nope. Just passing through. Chasing nothing."

Clyde raised his glass. "To chasing nothing."

She clinked it. "Have a drink on me."

By the fourth shot, they were swapping stories.

Clyde told her about the night he quit his band mid-set and walked out into the rain without his guitar.

She told him about walking out of a Vegas wedding, still in the dress, with the keys to his car.

Somewhere around midnight, Clyde reached into his bag and pulled out an unopened bottle—cheap bourbon, still sealed.

Monica looked at it like it was a holy relic.

"You planning to die tonight?" she asked softly.

Clyde stared at the bottle.

"Maybe."

She shook her head. "Not here, you're not. Too many ghosts already in this place."

He smirked. "You gonna save me?"

"I'm not here to save you," she said. "But I'll sit with you 'til the urge passes."

They drank some more... much more.

Laughed.

The jukebox belted out "Have a Drink on Me" like a defiant anthem, like a prayer for the damned.

When the bartender shouted "Last call!" Clyde didn't flinch.

Monica stood, stretched, and tossed some crumpled bills on the bar.

"You got anywhere to be?" she asked.

"No."

"Good," she said, walking toward the door. "Then you can buy me breakfast."

Clyde stared at the bottle in his hand.

Then he set it down, unopened.

He picked up the duffel bag and followed her out into the dry morning air, where the sun was already punching through the clouds like it meant it.

The End

ABOUT THE AUTHOR

JESUS J. TERAN is a Marine Corps Veteran and life-long musician. He has been a principal of several schools in El Paso, Texas. He earned a Master of Education degree from the University of Texas at El Paso. He is married to Hortencia "Tootsie" Teran, who is a Federal Agent. (He is the only person that calls her Tootsie, so she's probably going to be angry when she reads this.) He loves his children, grandkids, and his dog Sadie.

ABOUT THE AUTHOR